Judith Gorog

IN A MESSY, MESSY ROOM

Illustrated by

KIMBERLY BULCKEN ROOT

Philomel Books • New York

This book is for all of our favorite teachers and librarians,
the ones with messy desks and the ones
who don't understand about messy desks.
–JG

To Kris – KBR

Text copyright © 1990 by Judith Gorog.
Illustrations copyright © 1990 by Kimberly Bulcken Root.
Published by Philomel Books,
a division of The Putnam & Grosset Book Group,
200 Madison Avenue, New York, NY 10016.
Published simultaneously in Canada.
All rights reserved.
Book design by Golda Laurens.

Library of Congress Cataloging-in-Publication Data
Gorog, Judith. In a messy, messy room/by Judith Gorog. p.   cm.
Summary: A collection of scary stories with humorous
or unexpected endings.
1. Horror tales, American.   2. Children's stories, American.
[1. Horror stories.   2. Short stories.] I. Title.
P27.G673In   1990 [Fic]–dc20.   89-35623CIPAC
ISBN 0-399-22218-9

5   7   9   10   8   6

In a Messy, Messy Room—A Note

On a day when I was visiting a fifth grade class, someone asked me if I had written any scary funny stories for third graders. In the course of talking about reading and writing and storytelling with the fifth graders that day, I told most of the stories in this book, asking the fifth graders if they thought third graders would like them. Later I asked some eighth graders, some grown-ups, and finally, I asked third graders. They suggested that a book of scary funny stories also include a truly gross story, and so it does. The stories are meant to be read aloud and are easy to memorize for storytelling.

The Angel

BRUNO WAS a housewrecker. His father was a housewrecker, and so was his Uncle Joe. His mother was a housewrecker, and so was his Aunt Lil.

Bruno's family took old buildings apart. They took apart the inside of apartments, and apartment buildings, schools, and even factories, old houses, and once a castle that was being knocked down to make room for a freeway. Bruno's family saved the best pieces of old buildings by putting them on the family truck. They saved fences and gates, doors and doorways, even rainspouts when they were made of copper.

Carefully Bruno's family would drive their truck to the big black iron gates of The Yard. There, outside the gates, they stopped the truck. Bruno's favorite job was jumping out of the truck to swing open those huge gates, which were made to look like a giant garden of climbing roses. All the flowers, stems, leaves, and thorns of those gates were made from black iron. After the truck was inside The Yard, Bruno closed the big gates and helped unload the pieces.

Bruno worked in The Yard and played in The Yard. He lived in the house surrounded by The Yard. When he was only five years old, Bruno knew a lot about the parts of houses. He knew about pediments and pedestals. He knew about porticos and pillars and he knew how to take care of marble.

To a casual visitor, The Yard might look like the biggest jumble you ever saw. But Bruno knew every piece in it, and they all knew him. No one in Bruno's family found it the least bit strange when the mantelpiece of a fireplace sighed, or cried, or spoke. Everyone in the family listened when a rose window pleaded for a new home. But mostly the pieces in The Yard spoke to Bruno.

Of course, some of the pieces from old abandoned houses were sad and silent. But most of the pieces begged to be noticed. "Brunooo!" whispered a pair of carved window cornices, "please put us into an old house that is being repaired." "Bruno!" exclaimed the most decorated fireplace you ever saw, "put me into a clean and simple new house, pleeeeezzzzeeee!" Bruno listened when the pieces spoke. Bruno tried to help.

Bruno's whole family brought out treasures from the piles and heaps in The Yard. These they showed to the customers who bought the treasures and took them home to old houses and to new ones.

But of the whole family Bruno listened best and was most helpful. He led a family with six children to the elegant curved balustrade that had complained how it missed the daredevil banister sliders of the good old days. He led a sedate gentleman to a set of wall sconces that silently longed to be in a quiet reading room. Bruno helped the pieces that begged aloud for homes, and Bruno helped the quiet ones. Except.

Except for the Angel.

When Angel first came to The Yard, Bruno felt sure that Angel was going to be something special. Angel had one somewhat damaged wing,

the result of a bad fall. Angel's face was stern and beautiful. Bruno could have loved Angel.

Except.

Except.

Angel never said, "Please find me a home." No indeed. At first Angel just stood in The Yard looking down at Bruno when Bruno walked past.

Day after day Bruno smiled up at Angel. Grim Angel never said a word. Then, all at once, just when Bruno was not looking, Angel reached out. Angel touched Bruno's arm with one long, cold finger.

Bruno shivered.

Then Angel thundered, "BRUNO! PUT ME . . ."

Bruno, scared half out of his mind, ran away and stayed away from Angel all that day.

The next day, Bruno crept home from school. He made his way into The Yard by a path through the piles of decorative doorways. That path was far, far from where Angel stood. Then, when Bruno was just about to open the kitchen door, he felt Angel's cold, cold hand on his arm. Once again Angel commanded, "BRUNO! PUT ME OVER YOUR . . . !"

Bruno dropped his lunchbox and books. Too afraid of what Angel might be demanding, he ran like anything. Bruno's heart was halfway choking him in his throat. Bruno stayed away from The Yard all afternoon. He sneaked into the house for dinner. He stayed inside after dinner.

That night Bruno hid deep under the covers of his bed. At first he felt safe. But then, through all the blankets, he could hear Angel. "BRUNO! PUT ME OVER YOUR G . . ."

"Noooooooooooo," sang Bruno. He pulled the pillow over his head.

Bruno stuck his fingers into his ears. All night long Bruno sang. He sang song after song so that he could not hear the rest of the G word.

Bruno was sure he knew what Angel was going to say. Bruno was sure that Angel was demanding to be put over Bruno's GRAVE!

No way. Bruno told himself that if he did not hear what Angel said, then he would live. Bruno had to figure a way to escape from Angel. But how?

The next morning Bruno ran out of The Yard. Bruno ran all the way to school. All day long Bruno tried to think how he could escape from Angel. How could Bruno make sure that Angel never finished that sentence?

When school ended, Bruno walked home as slowly as it is possible for a human boy to walk. Still, the time came when Bruno saw the big black iron gates. Bruno was home.

Bruno looked to the right. No sign of Angel.

Bruno looked to the left. No sign of Angel.

Carefully Bruno crept up to the gate of The Yard.

Then, right next to the big iron front gate of The Yard, Angel suddenly appeared. Angel grabbed both Bruno's hands and held them so that Bruno could not put his fingers into his ears.

"BRUNO! BRUNO!" boomed the voice of Angel, "PUT   ME OVER   YOUR   GATE!"

So Bruno did.

THE FALLEN ANGEL SALVAGE YARD

Wet Kisses

Zack wasn't afraid of the creaking of the old ferryboat. He wasn't afraid of how it tipped to one side. He was never, ever scared when the water lapped, lapped all day and all night at the bottom of the boat.

Zack did not tremble when the wind made the rushes and reeds sigh outside. No, not even when the winter storms howled all the way down the rusty pink funnel, through the whole boat, into the bunk where Zack slept.

No. Zack liked living on the old mustard-yellow ferryboat aground in the weeds and water. Unka said that he and Zack were bachelors together. And mostly they were. Hardly anybody came all the way out to the old ferryboat on the marshes.

One person did.

Mrs. Beelzebub.

Then Zack was afraid.

Then Zack tried to hide.

Mrs. Beelzebub always found him.

He could hear her coming. That frizzled woman with the fat wet lips started calling long before she came into sight. "Zack! Ohhhh, Zackie. You darling boy! You're so cute I could eat you up!"

Up the gangplank she'd come, huffing and puffing. Up she'd come, licking her thick, wet lips. Straight for Zack she'd come, faster than she looked. If she caught him she'd pinch his cheeks. She'd give him wet kisses. And from the look in her eyes, Zack knew. One day she'd eat him up.

"Awww, Mizzus Bee. Let the boy be," Unka would say. "Havva cuppa coffee."

Mrs. Beelzebub never wanted to let Zack go.

Zack was always afraid. What if she came when Unka wasn't there to stop her? What if one day she didn't stop when Unka offered her coffee? What if he could never outrun her?

Zack tried. How he tried! He tried to guess when she'd show up. He ran faster. He found hiding places all over the boat. He found hiding places in the marshes.

But Zack never knew when his day would be ruined. How he dreaded that sound! How it sent chills down his spine!

"Ohhh, Zack! Zackieeee! You darling boy. I love your fat cheeks. You're so cute. I'll eat you uppppppp!"

The worst was, it didn't seem to bother Unka at all. One day Mrs. Beelzebub arrived when Zack was just about to make a really good move in checkers. Terrified, Zack jumped up from the game and ran like anything to hide.

And Unka? What did he do? He ambled over to make some coffee. Zack hardly made it out to the deck and around the corner before Mrs. Beelzebub grabbed him.

"Gotcha! Darling boy! Haaaaahhhaaa." Mrs. Beelzebub lifted Zack high in the air, kissed him with those wet lips. Zack struggled. Unka called, "Lettum be. Havva cuppa coffee, Mizzus Bee."

With one last wet kiss and one last hungry look, Mrs. Beelzebub let Zack go. Zack ran. He hid and did not come out even when Unka told him that she'd gone. Zack did not come even when Unka called him to finish the checkers game. Zack was that scared.

Zack knew it. He knew that one day she'd catch him alone. Zack dreaded the day.

Zack stuck to Unka closer than a shadow. Zack made sure he was never, ever home alone on the ferryboat on the lonely marshes. Zack practiced running fast and faster. Zack found hiding places everywhere. And Zack worried.

Worrying wore Zack out so that one morning he overslept. The sunlight coming straight into his eyes through the porthole, woke Zack up. He ran out to find Unka but saw only the rinsed-out coffee cup on the sink. Unka was gone.

A note said: "Need parts for the truck. BACK AT 4:00." It was eight-thirty in the morning. Could Zack make it through a whole day worrying about Mrs. Beelzebub coming there and finding him alone? No. He could not. Zack wrote his own note: "BACK AT 4:30." Zack would come home half an hour after Unka. That was safe. Unka never was late for anything.

Zack made three peanut butter and pickle sandwiches and put them into a bag. He added two apples then went to get his bicycle. Pushing the bike through the reeds and sand, Zack went to the road. He pedaled first to the playground, but no one was there. Zack ate his lonely lunch. From one friend's house to another Zack rode his bike, but no one was home. Then it started to rain. Zack looked at his watch. What a piece of junk! Even in the pouring rain Zack could see that his watch had stopped.

Cold, wet, and getting hungry again, Zack rode his bike back to the marshes. Pushing his bicycle along the path to the ferryboat, Zack looked carefully around him. No sign of Mrs. Beelzebub. That was good, but no sign of Unka either. Zack shivered. Zack pushed his bike under the gangplank, then peeked out. No sign of anyone. Zack ran inside to change his wet clothes.

It was 3:30 by the galley clock.

At 3:35 Zack heard the call.

"Zack!!! Ohh, Zackie!!!!" Zack ran.

CLOMP! CLOMP! CLOMP! Her clogs thumped on the gangplank. Zack darted into a locker under one of the benches on the main deck. Closing the lid, he buried himself under the moldy life jackets. Zack held his breath. She'd never find him there.

CLOMP! CLOMP!

She was on the captain's deck.

CLOMP!

Then a long silence.

Did Zack dare to hope she'd gone?

BANG! The lid of the locker crashed open!

There she was! Tossing aside the life vests, Mrs. Beelzebub hauled Zack out of the locker. Zack's fear froze him. There was nothing he could do. Mrs. Beelzebub lifted him up close to her face, close to those thick wet lips, and fixed him with her beady eyes.

"Ohh, Zack," she cried. "Zack . . . You've grown. You're not cute anymore."

Oh, Louis!!!

"Oh, Louis," said Great Aunt Smelda, bending down to give Louis a whiskery kiss on his cheek. "Oh, Louis," Great Aunt Smelda said again, "how you've grown. I'd never have recognized you!"

Louis waited politely until no one was looking before he rubbed his cheek where the prickly feeling was left by Great Aunt Smelda's whiskers.

Just thinking about what Great Aunt Smelda had said made Louis shudder, even though he knew Great Aunt Smelda was wrong. Even if he had grown, he still had the same green eyes. Even if he had grown, he still had the same brownish-red hair. And he still had the same mole in the same spot on his chin.

Nevertheless, whenever Great Aunt Smelda saw Louis, she always said, "Oh, Louis, how you've grown. I'd never have recognized you." And when she said it, Louis always felt scared, because he was a worrier.

It was easy for Louis to imagine his mother saying, "Oh, Louis. You're going off to Oslo to visit Aunt Freya. When you get there," Louis could imagine his mother saying, "you'll know Aunt Freya by the red umbrella she'll be carrying."

Louis could imagine his mother sending him off without another thought. Louis could imagine himself getting on the airplane all alone, knowing that Aunt Freya had not seen him since he was a baby.

He could imagine himself arriving at the airport in Oslo, terrified out of his mind that Aunt Freya would not recognize him. Louis could imagine the airport in Oslo. He could imagine himself, shaking at the knees, standing there all alone in the airport in Oslo–where everyone would be carrying a red umbrella!

But then out of the crowd would come Aunt Freya, her red-brown hair floating around her face, saying, "Oh, Louis. I'd know you anywhere!"

Louis could also imagine his father saying in a voice so calm it almost sounded bored, "Oh, Louis. You're taking a boat, and then a train, and then a camel ride to visit Uncle Otto in Timbuktu.

"You'll recognize Uncle Otto," Louis could imagine his father saying, "because he's as bald as an egg and always wears round eyeglasses."

Louis could imagine himself, terrified, trudging off to take a boat and a train, scared speechless. He could imagine hauling himself onto the back of a swaying camel to make his way to far-off Timbuktu. Louis could imagine that the closer he got, the more certain he'd be that Uncle Otto, who had not seen him in years, would never recognize him.

Then Louis could imagine that in hot Timbuktu there would be a huge crowd of people at the camel-unloading place, all of them wearing round sunglasses. All the people would have their heads covered with long cloths so that you could not tell who was bald and who wasn't.

But then, just when Louis would be faint with terror, someone would whip off his round sunglasses and say, "Hellllo, Louis. I'd recognize those green eyes anywhere!"

Or Louis would imagine his father *and* his mother saying, way, way too cheerfully, "Oh, Louis. You're going off to Iceland to see your cousins Snipp, Snapp, and Snurr.

"You'll know them because they are triplets who always dress alike, in blue shorts and gray jackets."

Off Louis would go to Iceland, scared to death because he'd never even met his cousins.

Louis could imagine himself arriving in Iceland, where the airport would be crammed to the bursting point with boys dressed alike in blue shorts and gray jackets. There would also be huge banners and signs in the airport that said:

WORLD'S LARGEST GATHERING OF TRIPLETS

MEETING OF THE BOY CHOIRS OF THE WORLD

Seeing all those boys, all wearing blue shorts and gray jackets, Louis would know for absolutely certain that he'd never, EVER find his cousins. He'd never seen these cousins!

But then out of the crowd would come three laughing boys, and Louis would laugh, too, because they'd all have eyes like his, and hair like his, and moles on their chins just as he did. The triplets and Louis would recognize each other immediately!

All this imagining of terrible, scary trips did not help Louis one bit on the morning when his mother really did say, "Louis, I have a nice surprise for you today. First we'll take your favorite train, the Dinky, from Princeton to Princeton Junction and then *you'll* take the train to New York. Great Aunt Smelda will meet you at the station. She has a nice surprise planned for you."

When his mother finished telling him, Louis looked stunned. "Excuse me, Mother," he replied. "What did you just say?" Louis's mother, in a very cheerful voice, repeated the plan. Louis was terrified.

Louis had always liked to ride the Dinky, and the idea of taking the train to New York usually filled him with joy. But, today Louis was panicked. Great Aunt Smelda would never ever recognize him! She never had.

Terrified, Louis dressed. Shaking with fear, he pretended to eat breakfast. Knees weak, he followed his mother to the car, sat there while she drove. Louis was green with fear, but his mother never noticed. Trembling, he got into the Dinky, rode without seeing the fields and woods alongside the tracks. His mouth too dry to swallow, he waved a weak good-bye to his mother from his seat on the train.

All the way to New York he worried about Great Aunt Smelda and what he would do when she did not recognize him. Maybe he could just ride home again. But maybe they'd make him get off the train. Maybe he'd be stuck there in the train station in New York City forever.

The trip was an agony of stops. They stopped for stations. Louis read the names: NEW BRUNSWICK, EDISON, RAHWAY. Nothing said PENN STATION. Then the train stopped at a place where a lot of tracks crossed. The ground outside was covered with trash, plastic coffee cups, ticket stubs, twisted wire. The train stayed there a long time. What if it stopped there forever? That wasn't a station. Then, slowly, the train crept forward. It stopped. The lights went out, then came on. The train creaked into a tunnel, stopped again.

Finally, after an agonizing time of stop-start-and-wait, the train groaned into Penn Station. At first Louis thought he was too scared to stand up. But he did. Crushed in the middle of a million tall grown-ups, he shuffled the length of the train car. Gulping for air and courage, he stood still. He was at the top of the steps on the platform between his car and the next one. Now he would have to get off the train. Louis raised his eyes from his feet.

There, at the door of his train car, stood Great Aunt Smelda, who held out her hand for him to shake. "Oh, Louis." she said. "Did you have a good trip?"

"Yeah!" said Louis. "It was terrific."

In a Messy, Messy Room

In a messy, messy room, at a messy, messy desk, sat a messy, messy boy named Sam.

In the daylight hours Sam loved his messy, messy room. His table, his bookcases, his walls were all covered with the things Sam saved. From the ceiling were hanging the white paper airplanes Sam made. Things tumbled out of boxes under Sam's table and bookcases. Things tumbled out of Sam's closet. Sam never threw anything away.

In the daylight hours Sam collected things. Sam built things. Sam looked at things. Sam read.

In the daylight hours nothing bothered Sam. It didn't bother Sam when
his father and mother,
his sisters and brothers,
his aunts and uncles and cousins,
his grandmothers and grandfathers
all looked in the door of Sam's room and groaned, "SAM! CLEAN YOUR ROOM!!!"

In the daylight hours Sam also liked to play hide-and-seek with his pet chameleon, Champ. Champ lived in an old, cracked aquarium on top of Sam's bookcase. Sam had put a layer of dirt and sand in the aquarium. Then he added some pieces of wood from the garden. Then he stuck in some leaves and branches. He covered the aquarium with a screened top. Every day Sam sprayed water into Champ's home. Every day Sam put insects or mealworms into Champ's home for Champ to eat. All day long Champ sat or ran in his home, changing colors and patterns as he went. By sitting very still and looking long and hard at the aquarium, Sam got pretty good at finding Champ hidden among the leaves and wood.

When night came, Champ disappeared. Even with the light on, Sam could not see Champ in the aquarium. When night came, and his room was dark, Sam got scared. In the dark, scurrying, scuttling sounds echoed in Sam's room. When night came, Sam put his teddy bear over the crack between his bed and the wall. Teddy could keep some scary things from coming up through the crack.

But what would keep the scary scratching noises away from Sam's room? Every night Sam tried to fall asleep somewhere else in the house. He offered to keep his sisters and brothers company while they studied. He offered to watch TV with anyone in the family. He asked to watch TV alone. After ten minutes in front of the TV, Sam always fell asleep.

If they said, "No TV," Sam tried to hide in the living room or the study. If no one noticed him, he would fall asleep somewhere else in the house, not in his own room. Then someone would carry Sam to his bed. Then lucky Sam would not have to try to fall asleep in his room with those scuttling sounds. Then lucky Sam could sleep until morning.

But sometimes unlucky Sam was sent to bed by everyone.

"Sam," they'd say, "clean your room and go to bed."

Poor Sam would quickly jump into his bed.

Scrabble. Scrabble.

Sam was so scared.

Sam would ask someone to read to him until he fell asleep.

Lucky Sam if someone did.

Scared Sam if no one did.

Scrabble. Scrabble.

One night scared Sam lay in his bed. He was trying hard to fall asleep before his mother finished reading to him. That way he'd never be alone with those scary sounds in his room. Then, long before Sam was asleep, his mother's voice stopped. Sam's eyes snapped open.

Scrabble. Scrabble.

Sam's mother was peering at Champ's glass aquarium with the screen on top. The scratching, scrabbling sounds that scared Sam were very loud in the room.

"What's that?" whispered Sam.

"Beetles," said Sam's mother. "Champ's aquarium is full of black beetles. Maybe they came in with the piece of rotten wood. Does Champ eat them?" she asked.

"I don't think so," said Sam, still scared, but thinking hard.

Poor old Champ. No wonder Sam never saw him at night. Champ must be hiding from those beetles. They must come out at night and hide very well during the day.

The next day Sam let Champ out of the glass aquarium into Sam's room. Champ ran around in Sam's room, changing colors and patterns as he ran through Sam's collections.

Sam wanted to play hide-and-seek with Champ, but first he had to get rid of the aquarium full of black beetles. Sam carried the aquarium down to the basement. He left it there, in the room full of all the cans of paint for painting the house. Sam went back up to his own room to play hide-and-seek with Champ.

What a relief. Now Sam's room would not be scary at night. For the first time he could remember, Sam went to bed that night in his own room without being afraid. He went the first time he was told to go to bed. He went without a struggle.

When Sam got to his room, he was disappointed because he could not find Champ anywhere. Still, Sam felt great. The black beetles were gone from his room. Sam sighed. Sam stretched out in his bed and closed his eyes.

Scrabble. Scrabble.

Under the covers, Sam started to shake. Sam's room echoed with scrabbling noises. Too scared to get out of bed, Sam lay awake and afraid.

Scrabble. Scrabble. Scrabble.

In the daylight hours Sam loved his messy, messy room. He built things and made things, and he and Champ had wonderful games of hide-and-seek. Sometimes Champ hid and Sam found him, and sometimes Sam hid and Champ found him.

But. As soon as it got dark, Sam could not find Champ. As soon as it got dark, Sam got scared. Sam remembered that scrabble-scrabble sound that happened in his room even after he had taken the aquarium full of scrabbling black beetles down to the basement. Since that night, Sam had not once tried to fall asleep in his own room. Sam had managed every single night since then to fall asleep somewhere else in the house so that someone would carry sleeping Sam into his bed.

*   *   *

But then the night came when the whole family told Sam to go up to bed in his own bed in his own room. "You are a big kid now," they all said. "Clean your room. And go to bed."

Terrified, Sam followed the path of moonlight to his bed. Shaking, Sam hid under his covers.

Scrabble. Scrabble. Scrabble.

One by one the rest of the family went to bed.

Scrabble. Scrabble. Scrabble.

Sam trembled.

Scrabble.

Scrabble.

Sam made himself as small as he could under the covers.

Something scrabbled on Sam's covers.

Something pulled the covers off Sam's head.

"Sam!" said a voice.

"Sam. I found you. Open your eyes."

Sam peeked. It was Champ, standing on the covers, changing colors and patterns in the moonlight.

"Sam," said Champ, "I *like* this messy, messy room!

"Never.

"Never.

"Never clean your room!"

Smelly Sneakers

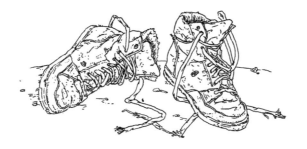

Only his mother and father called him Todd.

To every kid in town the name Todd suggested just one nickname, "Toad," which Toad didn't mind at all. You see, Toad wanted, more than anything else in the world, to win the smelly-sneaker contest.

Toad's sneakers were smelly. No doubt of that. But the first year he entered the contest, he didn't even get third prize.

The second year Toad entered the smelly-sneaker contest, he worked hard at it all year. He had already learned from the older kids that not wearing sox mattered. By not wearing sox, Toad made his sneakers much, much smellier. In addition, Toad fudged on his showers. He turned on the water. He more or less got into the shower and more or less washed most of himself, including his hair. He knew his mom and dad could tell the difference between the smell of clean hair and the smell of dirty hair, but they trusted him to wash his feet. Toad did not wash his feet, which helped the smell of his sneakers considerably.

Still, that second year Toad got only second place.

Toad was bitterly disappointed. After the contest, he stood sad and dejected by a large garbage can, trying to decide if he should just chuck those second-place sneakers right into the garbage.

"Hey, kid!" called a hoarse voice from the other side of the can.

"Hey, kid!!!" the voice insisted.

"Yeah?" said Toad.

"How much you wanna win that contest?"

"More than anything!" said Toad.

"I know how you can win," said the voice.

Toad peered around the garbage can, where a big skinny kid sat on the ground.

"What'll ya give me if I tell?"

Without hesitation, Toad offered his high-tech skateboard, the thing he loved most, the one he'd earned, a skateboard with super trucks. He'd give the skateboard he'd painted himself, put rails on, used every day. Toad offered it to the kid sitting beside the garbage can.

"Here's what ya do," said the kid, and he whispered instructions into Toad's ear, then put a small vial into Toad's hand.

"Thanks," said Toad.

The kid stood up, shrugged.

With a smile of pure delight, Toad offered the tall skinny kid his skateboard, but the kid turned his back. "Awww . . . Keep it," was all he said.

Toad raced home. The contest rules said you had to start the year with a clean pair of sneakers. Some kids tried to cheat, but not Toad. He was sure he'd win, for in that vial was essence of sneaker, foot sweat mixed with scrapings from the sneakers of the last four winners of the Great Smelly Sneaker Contest grand prize. Toad put the precious droplets into his new sneakers. The results were instant and made Toad's eyes water.

All that year he went sockless and put plastic bags on his sneakers at

night to keep the smell in, even though his parents made him put the sneakers outside. After a few days, his teachers, too, insisted that Toad's sneakers be left outside. Toad did as the teachers said, first bagging the sneakers to keep the concentrated smell from getting diluted.

Toad's dedication and hard work paid off. As the day of the Great Smelly Sneaker Contest drew closer, it was clear to everyone in town that Toad would be the winner.

The first judge approached Toad's sneakers. From more than a yard away, he began to retch.

The second judge wiped her eyes, waved a sheaf of papers before her face, and backed away from Toad's sneakers.

The third judge took a whiff, grinned, and said, "Now that's more like it!" and awarded Toad first prize!

Toad was giddy with bliss. When the judges asked if he'd like to donate the sneakers to the museum, Toad said no. He'd wear them home. He'd savor being champion.

Off Toad went, right foot, left foot, wearing championship sneakers, ones you could smell from afar. Right foot. Left foot.

Toad was a good long way from home when his left foot started to itch something awful right around his toes, but Toad did not stop to scratch. He went on and on. And it was not long before his right foot started to itch something fierce right around his toes, but Toad kept on walking.

And he walked and he walked and the itch got to itching the whole sole of his right foot and then the whole sole of his left foot.

But Toad kept on walking, without stopping to scratch until he got home. And the itching was terrible—clear up to his ankles!

With a sigh of relief Toad got home and reached down to take off his championship smelly sneakers.

But when Toad took off the championship smelly sneakers and got ready to scratch, Toad discovered that

his

feet

were

gone.